BILL COSBY

LITTLE **BILL** BOOKS FOR BEGINNING READERS

Money Troubles

by Bill Cosby

Illustrated by Varnette P. Honeywood

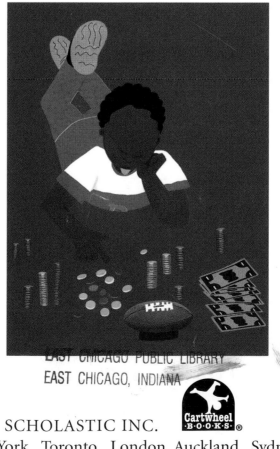

SCHOLASTIC INC.

Cartwheel ·B·O·O·K·S·®

New York   Toronto   London   Auckland   Sydney

Assistants to art production: Rick Schwab, Nick Naclerio

Copyright © 1998 by Bill Cosby.
All rights reserved. Published by Scholastic Inc.
CARTWHEEL BOOKS and the CARTWHEEL BOOKS logo
are trademarks and/or registered trademarks of Scholastic Inc.

Library of Congress Cataloging-in-Publication Data

Cosby, Bill, 1937-
    Money troubles / Bill Cosby ; illustrated by Varnette P. Honeywood.
      p.   cm.— (A little Bill book)
    "Cartwheel books."
    Summary: While trying to raise enough money for a telescope, Little Bill makes a discovery about generosity and the needs of others.
    ISBN 0-590-16402-3 (hardcover)   0-590-95623-X (paperback)
    [1. Moneymaking projects — Fiction. 2. Generosity — Fiction. 3. Afro-Americans — Fiction.]
    I. Honeywood, Varnette P., ill. II. Title. III. Series. IV. Series: Cosby, Bill, 1937- Little Bill book.
PZ7.C8185Mo   1998
[Fic] — dc21   97-34106
                                                           CIP
                                                           AC

10 9 8 7 6 5 4 3 2 1   8 9/9 0/0 01 02

Printed in the U.S.A.   23
First printing, June 1998

To Ennis,
"Hello, friend,"
B.C.

To the Cosby Family,
Ennis's perseverance against the odds
is an inspiration to us all,
V.P.H.

Dear Parent:

One of the best ways children learn about the value and significance of money is through regular saving. Even small children appreciate the purpose of saving when they can buy toys with money from their piggy banks.

Eventually, children realize that *working* brings in money. To reinforce this important feature of the real world, some parents pay young children to do chores around the house as well as give them an allowance. Many parents, to discourage materialism, also encourage their children to donate some small amount of their savings to good causes.

Older children, like Little Bill, find they can also earn money through jobs outside the family. In *Money Troubles*, Little Bill is inspired to buy a telescope after learning about astronomy in school. (Not, it must be said, because he's suddenly become a serious scholar. Instead, he dreams of becoming famous. He'll discover a new comet, and it will be named after him.) The telescope he wants costs $100; he has $47.87 in his bank. To start earning the rest, he washes a neighbor's car, then collects cans and bottles—until he notices another boy, obviously poor, also out scavenging. Little Bill leaves his own cans where the other boy will find them.

Little Bill has realized something important: other people may need money more than he does. He takes this lesson further by dropping the telescope idea, donating all his savings to the school's food drive for the poor…and becoming "famous" for contributing the most food.

Through his unselfish acts, Little Bill has learned that giving to others can be more satisfying than acquiring a possession he can do without. And he has taken an important step toward understanding what it means to be part of a community.

Alvin F. Poussaint, M.D.
Clinical Professor of Psychiatry,
Harvard Medical School and
Judge Baker Children's Center,
Boston, MA

Chapter One

Hello, friend. My name is Little Bill and I am going to be famous. I'll tell you why. Do you want to know what I like to do? I like to look at the night sky. I do!

Way out there — way past Pluto — is the Oort Cloud. It looks like a cloud because it is made up of billions of comets. Billions.

My teacher, Miss Murray, said so.
And she said maybe one day, one of
those comets will pull away from the
Oort Cloud. It will travel through
space toward the sun.

And one day, when I'm looking up
at the sky, I'll see that comet. And
maybe I'll be *the first person ever* to

see that comet. I'll run and call the people who give names to comets. I'll tell them my name and what I saw.

Then they'll say, "Congratulations!" And they'll name it Comet Little Bill. I'll be famous! Yessss! But first, I need a telescope.

Chapter Two

I was shooting hoops in the driveway. Ms. Hernandez, our mail carrier, came by.

"I'll take it, Ms. Hernandez," I said.

There were lots of letters for Mom and Dad, a magazine for my brother Bobby, and some catalogs.

On the back of a catalog, I saw what I wanted — a telescope.

There was one *big* problem. It cost $100! Mom and Dad would never give me $100! There was only one thing for me to do. I had to get the money myself.

I already had some money in my football bank.

Some of the money was from Aunt Martha. She gave me a dollar when she came for a visit.

"Spend it wisely," she said.

Some of the money was from Uncle Joe.

"Enjoy it," he said.

Some of the money was from the tooth fairy.

I opened a little door on the bank and shook it. All the dollars, quarters, dimes, nickels, and pennies dropped out. An old stick of gum fell out, too.

I counted 34 dollar bills, 21 quarters, 53 dimes, 39 nickels, 137 pennies — and 1 old stick of gum.

I added all the dollars, quarters, dimes, nickels, and pennies. It took a long time. I had $47.87. I only needed $52.13 more and I could buy my telescope. I only needed $52.13 and I could be famous!

Chapter Three

On Saturday morning, I dressed quickly. I ran to the kitchen.

"What's the rush?" Dad asked.

"I have to get a job," I said.

Dad laughed. "What else is new?"

My father started to get cereal from the cabinet.

"Wait!" I said.

"Wait what?" Dad asked.

"I'll get breakfast for you," I said.

Dad closed the cabinet door. "Well, thank you."

"How much will you pay me for getting your breakfast?"

"WHAT?" said Dad.

"Dad, I need a job."

Dad opened the cabinet door again. "I'll get my own cereal, thank you," said Dad.

I poured myself some cereal, too.

"Dad," I asked, "when you were my age, what did you do to make money?"

Dad leaned back in his chair. He looked up at the ceiling and smiled. Dad liked to think about the days when he was a boy.

"I used to deliver newspapers," he said, "but that was when I was older.

I used to collect empty bottles. I returned them to the store for the deposits. And I used to wash cars."

"Wash cars! What a great idea!" I said.

I started to run out of the house.

"Wait!" said Dad. "Your first job today is to put your spoon and bowl into the dishwasher — FREE OF CHARGE!"

Our neighbor, Mrs. Rizzo, lived by herself. She was happy when I offered to wash the car. "I usually take it to the car wash," she said. "But I hope you'll do a better job."

I helped my father wash his car many times, so I knew what to do. I wet the car with a hose. Then I filled a bucket with soapy water.

I washed every part: the doors, the hood, the trunk, the bumpers, the lights — even the wheels and the hubcaps. I had to jump up to reach the high parts.

Then I carried out Mrs. Rizzo's vacuum cleaner and vacuumed everything inside. I even vacuumed inside the trunk!

Mrs. Rizzo gave me rags for drying the car. I was tired, but the car looked pretty.

"It looks good," Mrs. Rizzo said. "Now you wax."

WAX?!!!

Waxing was even harder than washing. I put the wax on the car. Then I rubbed and rubbed. I had waxed half the car when Mrs. Rizzo gave me a peanut butter and jelly sandwich for lunch.

I finally finished waxing the car
and Mrs. Rizzo gave me $5. Only
$5? I was hoping for more. I should
have set a price before starting.

Andrew and José walked by with
a basketball. "Do you want to shoot
some hoops?" Andrew asked.

I wanted to play, but I was too
tired. "Later," I said, and I walked
into my house. The clock said 3:15.
I had worked almost all day, and I
still needed $47.13!

Chapter Four

A soda can was on the table. I read the side of the label. "5¢ deposit!" I grabbed the can. Dad's voice boomed, "I'M DRINKING THAT!"

"Sorry, Dad," I said.

I waited for him to finish so I could have the can. You know, my father is the slowest soda drinker in the world.

"You need a haircut," said Mom.
"Here's ten dollars. I want you to go
to Mr. Yoshi and get your hair cut
right now."

"But I have work to do," I said.

"Haircut first, work second," said
Dad.

Dad put his empty can in a big
plastic bag for me. Ready to start
my next job, I went out the door.
Collecting bottles and cans had to
be easier than washing cars. But I
had to get a haircut first.

On the way to Mr. Yoshi's shop,
I passed the school yard. I was in
luck. A soda can lay next to the goal
on the soccer field. I picked it up.
That's five cents, I said to myself.
I searched the rest of the field and
found more cans!

I saw another can next to a bush. I ran to get it. Zoom! It was gone. Behind the bush was a boy. He held two big bags. He must have had a hundred cans!

I ran to the playground to look for cans there. The boy ran to the handball courts. I found one can. The boy found a can, too. We both ran to the trash basket. I got there first.

I got to see the boy close-up. His clothes were dirty and torn. His shoes were worn-down and had holes. His eyes were kind of sad but they moved fast, looking for more cans.

That boy needed the cans more than I did. I left my cans next to the trash basket and walked away.

I walked over to the basketball courts. Andrew, José, Michael, and Fuchsia were there. "Are you ready to play?" Andrew asked. I still wanted to play. But I was supposed to get a haircut. And I still needed $47.13. Then I smiled. I had a great idea!

"Who knows how to cut hair?"

"I do," said Andrew.

"I'll give you two dollars to cut mine," I said.

I thought that I could spend two dollars on my haircut and keep eight dollars for my telescope!

We all went over to Andrew's house. We crowded into his bathroom. I couldn't even see the mirror. Fuchsia, Michael, and José kept telling Andrew things like "It's lopsided," or "Take a little more off over here."

Andrew cut and cut. When he
was done, I looked at Fuchsia,
Michael, and José. I read the bad
news on their faces. I was afraid to
look in the mirror.

"You don't have to pay me,"
Andrew said.

I didn't have to look in the mirror
to know that I had a very ugly
haircut.

Chapter Five

First, Mom and Dad looked mad. Then they laughed. Even my great-grandmother, Alice the Great, laughed at me. I wished that they would stop laughing and be mad again. When Bobby came home, he laughed too.

"Mr. Yoshi is closed tomorrow," Bobby said. "You'll have to go to church with that ugly hairdo."

"Does Mr. Yoshi open his shop before school on Monday?" I asked.

"I'm afraid not," Mom said. "You'll have to go to school, then go to see Mr. Yoshi at three o'clock."

"I'll wear a hat all day—even in church," I said.

Dad came to the rescue. He was holding clippers. Dad shaved off what was left of my hair. I looked in the mirror. "I like it!" I said.

Everyone cheered.

On Monday, the kids in school seemed to like my new haircut. While they were looking at me, I was looking at a sign for our food drive. Our school was collecting food for poor people.

Many people had bigger money troubles than mine — people like the boy who collected cans.

After school, I took the money from Mrs. Rizzo and the money from my bank. I went to the store and bought noodles, beans, and soup for the food drive.

I still want to be famous. I still want to have a comet named after me. But first, I want everyone to have food.

The next day we had an assembly. The principal, Ms. Woods, spoke to us.

"You boys and girls have given more food to the food drive this year than ever before," she said. "And Little Bill gave the most food of all!"

The kids clapped their hands. Andrew rubbed my head.

I was surprised when Ms. Woods said my name. Then I got another surprise. My picture was on the bulletin board! The words under my picture were:

GOOD CITIZEN, LITTLE BILL.

I guess I'm famous after all!

HOWARD L. BINGHAM

HOWARD L. BINGHAM

Bill Cosby is one of America's best-loved storytellers, known for his work as a comedian, actor, and producer. His books for adults include *Fatherhood*, *Time Flies*, *Love and Marriage*, and *Childhood*. Mr. Cosby holds a doctoral degree in education from the University of Massachusetts.

Varnette P. Honeywood, a graduate of Spelman College and the University of Southern California, is a Los Angeles-based fine artist. Her work is included in many collections throughout the United States and Africa.

Books in the LITTLE BILL series:

The Meanest Thing to Say
Can Little Bill be a winner...
and be nice, too?

The Treasure Hunt
Little Bill searches
for his best treasure.
What he finds is a great big surprise!

The Best Way to Play
How can Little Bill and his
friends have fun without the
new *Space Explorers* video game?

Super-Fine Valentine
The other boys are saying
that Little Bill is in love.
How can he stop them?

Shipwreck Saturday
Little Bill is proud of his
new boat. He made it himself.
But the older boys say it will sink!

Money Troubles
Little Bill needs $100.
How will he get it?

RAP

11-19-98